Pher

What Can I Bee?
I Wannabee a
FIREFIGHTER!

Written by
Amy Culliford

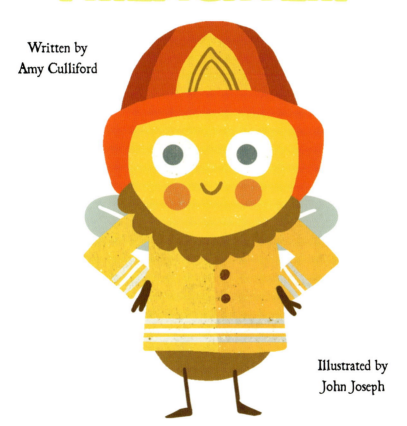

Illustrated by
John Joseph

A Blossoms Beginning Readers Book

CRABTREE
Publishing Company
www.crabtreebooks.com

BLOSSOMS BEGINNING READERS LEVEL GUIDE

Level 1 Early Emergent Readers Grades PK-K
Books at this level have strong picture support with carefully controlled text and repetitive patterns. They feature a limited number of words on each page and large, easy-to-read print.

Level 2 Emergent Readers Grade 1
Books at this level have a more complex sentence structure and more lines of text per page. They depend less on repetitive patterns and pictures. Familiar topics are explored, but with greater depth.

Level 3 Early Readers Grade 2
Books at this level are carefully developed to tell a great story, but in a format that children are able to read and enjoy by themselves. They feature familiar vocabulary and appealing illustrations.

Level 4 Fluent Readers Grade 3
Books at this level have more text and use challenging vocabulary. They explore less familiar topics and continue to help refine and strengthen reading skills to get ready for chapter books.

School-to-Home Support for Caregivers and Teachers

This book helps children grow by letting them practice reading. Here are a few guiding questions to help the reader with building his or her comprehension skills. Possible answers appear here in red.

Before Reading:
• What do I think this story will be about?
  • *I think this story will be about a bee who wants to be a firefighter.*
  • *I think this story will be about what it takes to be a firefighter.*

During Reading:
• Pause and look at the words and pictures. Why did the character do that?
  • *I think the bee wants to be a firefighter so he could help people.*
  • *I think the bee climbs a ladder to save a cat that is stuck in a tree.*

After Reading:
• Describe your favorite part of the story.
  • *My favorite part was when the bee saved the cat in the tree!*
  • *I liked seeing the bee driving around in a fire truck.*

What could I be?

3

I could be a
firefighter!

I could ride in a red fire truck.

I could use a hose.

I could go up and down ladders.

I could help people.

WRITING PROMPTS

Possible answers appear here in red.

1. **Write a different ending to the story.**

The bee decides fighting fires means he's always too warm, so he decides to be a lifeguard instead.

2. **Choose a character and write the story from that character's point of view.**

The cat decided it would be a good idea to climb the tree, until it got stuck and had to be saved by a firefighter!

3. **Write about a similar situation that you experienced.**

During the summer I felt like a firefighter when I used a water hose to put out our campfire.

ABOUT THE AUTHOR

Amy Culliford has been involved in the arts her entire life. After completing a Bachelor of Fine Arts degree at the University of Victoria, she worked for several years as a drama teacher in classrooms and after school programs. Presently, Amy works for a professional opera company by day, writes children's books by night, and performs as a princess at children's birthday parties on weekends. If she has any spare time, she likes to spend it planning her next trip to Disneyland!

ABOUT THE ILLUSTRATOR

John Joseph's passion for art appeared at an early age, while living in Orlando, Florida. As a young boy, he was inspired by his many trips to visit the animation studios just down the road, at the happiest place on Earth. It was very rare that you would spot him without a pencil and sketchbook, creating stories and drawing away.

John Joseph's love of art continued through school, and he went on to get an art education degree from Colorado State University and a masters degree from Lesley University. You could say that John has never really left school, as he graduated and went straight back to elementary school to teach visual arts. He is constantly inspired by the imagination of his students, and often includes them in his stories and illustrations.

Written by: Amy Culliford
Illustrations by: John Joseph
Art direction and layout by:
Under the Oaks Media
Series Development: James Earley
Proofreader: Kathy Middleton
Educational Consultant:
Marie Lemke M.Ed.
Print and production coordinator:
Katherine Berti

Library and Archives Canada Cataloguing in Publication

Title: I wannabee a firefighter! / written by Amy Culliford ;
    illustrated by John Joseph.
Names: Culliford, Amy, 1992- author. | Joseph, John, 1985- illustrator.
Description: Series statement: What can I bee? | "A blossoms
    beginning readers book".
Identifiers: Canadiana (print) 20210225955 |
    Canadiana (ebook) 20210225963 |
    ISBN 9781427153760 (hardcover) |
    ISBN 9781427153821 (softcover) |
    ISBN 9781427153883 (HTML) |
    ISBN 9781427153944 (EPUB) |
    ISBN 9781427154002 (read-along ebook)
Subjects: LCSH: Readers (Primary) | LCSH: Fire fighters—
    Juvenile literature. | LCSH: Fire extinction—Juvenile literature. |
    LCGFT: Readers (Publications)
Classification: LCC PE1119.2 .C87 2022 | DDC j428.6—dc23

Library of Congress Cataloging-in-Publication Data

Names: Culliford, Amy, 1992- author. | Joseph, John, 1985- illustrator.
Title: I wannabee a firefighter! / written by Amy Culliford ; illustrated
    by John Joseph.
Description: New York, NY : Crabtree Publishing Company, [2022]
    | Series What can I bee?
Identifiers: LCCN 2021023527 (print) |
    LCCN 2021023528 (ebook) |
    ISBN 9781427153760 (hardcover) |
    ISBN 9781427153821 (paperback) |
    ISBN 9781427153883 (ebook) |
    ISBN 9781427153944 (epub) |
    ISBN 9781427154002
Subjects: LCSH: Readers (Primary) | Fire fighters--Juvenile fiction. |
    LCGFT: Readers (Publications) | Picture books.
Classification: LCC PE1119.2 .C857 2022 (print) | LCC PE1119.2
    (ebook) | DDC 428.6/2--dc23
LC record available at https://lccn.loc.gov/2021023527
LC ebook record available at https://lccn.loc.gov/2021023528

Crabtree Publishing Company

www.crabtreebooks.com   1-800-387-7650

Printed in the U.S.A./072021/CG20210514

Published in the United States
Crabtree Publishing
347 Fifth Avenue, Suite 1402-145
New York, NY, 10016

Published in Canada
Crabtree Publishing
616 Welland Ave.
St. Catharines, ON, L2M 5V6

16